T0131809

LIFE WITH BRYCE

The Beginning: A Mother's Love

BLUE WALLS

AuthorHouse™
1663 Liberty Drive
Bloomington, IN 47403
www.authorhouse.com
Phone: 1 (800) 839-8640

© *2018 Blue Walls. All rights reserved.*

No part of this book may be reproduced, stored in a retrieval system,
or transmitted by any means without the written permission of the author.

Published by AuthorHouse 06/14/2018

ISBN: 978-1-5462-4645-9 (sc)
ISBN: 978-1-5462-4646-6 (e)

Print information available on the last page.

Any people depicted in stock imagery provided by Getty Images are models,
and such images are being used for illustrative purposes only.
Certain stock imagery © Getty Images.

This book is printed on acid-free paper.

Because of the dynamic nature of the Internet, any web addresses or links contained in this book may have changed
since publication and may no longer be valid. The views expressed in this work are solely those of the author and do not
necessarily reflect the views of the publisher, and the publisher hereby disclaims any responsibility for them.

authorHOUSE®

FOREWORD

It was a beautiful morning in Woodbridge, Virginia. The sun was rising in the east; not a cloud in sight. The birds were chirping excitedly, and before long, the kids would go out to play games and enjoy each other's company. They would laugh, dance, throw a ball, play tag, or just run, as kids are known to do. However, not all kids participated in these activities. Some kids just preferred to play alone and stay indoors.

This book is about one such boy. Though he was physically able, Bryce Johnson did not take part in most outdoor children's activities through no fault of his own. As a very young child without siblings, Bryce fell prey to unhealthy eating habits, and soon became a victim of childhood obesity. His parents were having their own problems, and neglected to address what Bryce was going through. He felt all alone, and eventually preferred it that way. To keep him happy and occupied, his parents were sure to give him whatever he wanted, and that usually resulted in his favorite snacks of ice cream, donuts, potato chips, and pretty much any kind of candy. His weight increased seemingly overnight, as his outdoor activities decreased, and his craving for snacks increased. What could easily have been a sad story of a depressed lonely kid, somehow became an uplifting tale of a young lad facing and accepting the challenges of his young life.

CHAPTER ONE

Bryce Johnson sat in silence. He thought about all the things that had happened to him in his young life. About how meeting Brooke and Micah helped change his life, and how they became his two best friends in the whole world. They meant the world to him. They weren't just his best friends; at one time they were his ONLY friends. At such a young age, having friends, or at least one friend, was a major deal. Before meeting Brooke and Micah, Bryce was pretty much a loner. He had no siblings, and making matters worse, he had a bit of a weight problem, and a huge lack of self-confidence. The fact that his overprotective mom and dad divorced when he was very young didn't help.

Bryce's mom and dad argued a lot during his early years. It was a time when he, as a single child, needed nurturing and encouragement most; however, there was little interaction between them, and Bryce spent most of his days and nights with his toys, playing video games, and watching TV. The problems his parents were having took center stage in their lives. They were attentive to Bryce, making sure he ate, and had plenty to do in his room. However, it was during this period as a young child that his weight gain began, basically unnoticed; and his self-confidence plummeted.

Prior to their divorce, Bryce's mom and dad tried for years to get him involved in local activities, but nothing ever seemed to work out. They signed him up for the Boy Scouts, soccer, and t-ball; and although Bryce loved playing, he was never any good, and his weight made it difficult for him to get around the field, and participate in children's activities. He'd never really interacted with other kids on that level, and immediately noticed that they could do things that he could not. He was not as fast or as strong or as physically gifted as some of the other kids.

Still, he had loads of fun playing with them. Eventually, the problems his parents were having begun to overshadow Bryce's ability to participate, as he missed practices, games, and just the opportunities available to a young child searching to find something special to be a part of.

For the next year or so, Bryce spent lots of time at his home, or out shopping with his mom. He remembers visiting relatives in North Carolina, but spent most of the time hanging onto, and around his mom; something he found most comforting and reassuring. Before the divorce, his dad spent more and more time away from home, and never really had much time for Bryce when he was there. There were times when Bryce asked his dad to show him how to catch a baseball; or dribble a basketball; or throw a football. His dad always told him he would, but never found the time. Bryce didn't really understand, but knew that the problems his parents were having really affected both his mom and dad. As his dad moved farther from them, physically and emotionally, Bryce and his mom grow that much closer. As a young child without siblings or a constant father figure, his mom was his world. She was always there for him. He would often awaken from a bad dream, and end up sleeping in her bed. By age 5, his dad was almost nonexistent in his life, and his mom found herself working extremely hard to be both mom and dad. Bryce was just happy to know that his mom was starting to move on with her life, and not crying at night, as she so often did in the past. He was happy, because his mom was happy. Things were finally starting to look good for Bryce and his mom.

During the summer before he would start first grade, Bryce's mom really took notice of his weight, and seriously thought about how that could affect him in school, his health, and maybe impact him socially.

She had basically "spoiled" him with anything he wanted, or at least most of the things he wanted. She couldn't stand to say no to him, especially with the way things happened with his dad. She felt guilty, and a little responsible for Bryce not having any real friends, and especially for his weight gain.

She knew she was all he had, and didn't want him to feel any more pangs of rejection. However, with school on the horizon, she knew how things could be difficult for him. Particularly with his peers. She had to act, and she had to be firm with Bryce. She could never forgive herself if he became the butt of jokes in school, or cried because of being ridiculed by other kids.

That summer, the first step was a heart-to-heart talk with her baby. "Bryce", she said. "Mommy loves you so much. I want you to be healthy, and part of that is eating healthy, and exercising so you can maybe lose weight, and be able to run and play with the other kids." She didn't know what his reaction would be, but was quite happy when he said "ok mommy".

First step, she thought, build his confidence. Help him to be sure of himself, and not be overly concerned about what others think. That is so important, Kim thought. Next would be to lose the weight; and finally, be able to defend himself from any kids who might want to bully him. After going toe-to-toe arguing with Bryce's dad almost daily for nearly 2 years, Kim Johnson had become seasoned at the art of confrontation, and promised herself she would never back down when it came to protecting and defending her child. Just to be clear, she was sure to tell him that fighting was never the best solution, and to avoid it when possible. Although she knew that with kids, it could very well come to that.

The start of school was just over a month away. Bryce never attended kindergarten, and was getting really excited about starting first grade. Kim, however, was the apprehensive parent. She had mixed emotions.

It was great he was finally starting school, and having the chance to interact with his teacher, as well as classmates; however, she wasn't sure how he'd be received by his peers, and mostly that she wouldn't be there to comfort him when, or if he needed her.

She knew he'd have to grow up and figure some things out on his own, but she wasn't ready for that. Not just yet. He was still her baby.

Bryce was such a sweet boy. When his mom and dad would argue, he'd usually go to his room and take out his toy soldiers and pretend they were in battle, and he was the leader. His group always won. He didn't really understand what the fuss between his parents was all about, but knew they mentioned his name often. He hoped that they weren't arguing about him. He hadn't done anything! He remembered asking his mom once if he'd done anything bad, and she assured him that he had not. So that was that. When she had time, his mom would take him to the local playground to hopefully play and interact with other kids his age. Going to the park was his most enjoyable time of the day. Although the swings were his favorite, he'd often marvel at the older kids playing basketball on the outdoor court, and wonder how they could be so good at it. There were kids throwing and catching a football, and others throwing a baseball around. How can they do that? He wondered. He would watch them for hours; play on the swings and in the sandbox, and then watch them some more. Kim was happy that Bryce seemed to show an interest in sports. She wasn't so sure after things went sour with t-ball and soccer. Maybe if Bill had spent more time with him… Well, no need wondering about that now. Bill's gone, and her son needs direction. She asked him one day why he enjoyed watching the older kids playing. "I just do", he replied. "Would you like to play like them one day?" she asked. "Well… dad was supposed to show me how, but he never had time."

"Maybe I can show you how. What do you think of that?" his mom asked. They both laughed at the thought. However, Kim was not joking. At that very moment she realized that this was a breakthrough of sorts, and her vastly overweight 6 year old son had just shown an interest in something real! She could hardly contain herself.

Why hadn't she thought of this before? I guess her issues with Bill consumed her, and she wasn't able to think about much else. Now that all of her focus was now on Bryce, she understood how their adult problems had as much impact on him, as it did them. She never thought of herself as selfish, but during the entirety of her separation and divorce from Bill, that's what she was. She was grateful that it appeared Bryce had not suffered any mental strain from the whole ordeal. At least not up to this point. She vowed to do better by him.

CHAPTER TWO

Kim Johnson was a stay-at-home mom by choice. At less than 30 years old, and a college graduate, she knew one day she'd have time to start and focus on a career. However, her immediate plans were placed on hold when she became pregnant with Bryce. She wanted her new baby to be her world. Hers and Bill's. She would stay home and care for her small family until Bryce started school. Then she would take a look at her options.

Kim and Bill both agreed that this was a great plan. Unfortunately, their problems became more than either could handle, and their separation, and ultimate divorce was imminent.

Now Bryce is 6 years old and getting ready for first grade. He lives alone with his mom. He knows he has a problem with eating too much, and exercising very little. Best that he could remember, whenever he felt really upset or depressed, eating was always the best therapy. He really enjoyed chocolate cupcakes and candy. Any kind of candy. Potato chips were his favorites as well. He could remember sitting in his room alone; watching TV or playing with his toys; and having a snack close by. This happened regularly. He didn't have to wonder why or how he'd become so large. He knew why. He found so much comfort in eating, and not doing much of anything else in his room. His favorite things were playing in his room, hanging with his mom, and eating. And not necessarily in that order.

He remembers a confrontation with his dad about a year or so prior, following one of Bill's many arguments with Kim. Bill wanted Bryce to get his toys out of the living room. Bryce apparently wasn't moving fast enough – for whatever reason; and Bill yelled for him to "move your fat butt!!" Everything froze at that moment. Kim gasped… Bryce stared at his dad. He was filled with both embarrassment and surprise. Dad had never talked to me this way, he thought. He called me fat! "Oh, I'm sorry Buddy. I didn't mean it…" said Bill. He was visibly upset at Kim, and remorseful regarding his comment to Bryce. However, the damage was done. From that point, Bryce's self-confidence was extremely low. Because of his lack of direct interaction with other kids, he never felt the pain of being ridiculed. Hearing it from his own dad was troubling. If there was ever a doubt, it was just confirmed. He was fat.

Kim knew that the time was now. School started in just over a month, and she wanted her son Bryce to lose weight and become more physically active. She had been a decent athlete in high school and college, and always managed to keep her body in pretty good shape. Which was surprising to her that she didn't see this coming. What to do, she thought. She needed a plan. A plan that Bryce wouldn't mind, and hopefully a plan that would be fun for him. She checked numerous websites to find out what was recommended. Through her research, she quickly discovered that she'd been far more concerned with Bryce's social standing, and less about his health. Whatever her plan, it needed to be safe, and not too demanding of him physically. His eating habits would have to change; particularly his snacking. He's not gonna be happy about that, she thought. But a moms gotta do what a moms gotta do…

CHAPTER THREE

The morning was frigid for a summer day. Kim would start a new job in September, so she had lots of time to spend with Bryce before school started. First thing that morning, she and Bryce shared a bowl of fruit - something she had picked up at the local food mart - and toast. And of course, his daily multi-vitamin. He loved it. "Can I have jelly on the toast mom?" he asked. "Uhh… sure Honey. Can't hurt".

After breakfast, Kim donned a pair shorts and a sweatshirt, and headed to the track at the local park to run a few laps. Bryce closely by her side. Before they left, she had him grab the bat, ball, and glove he kept from t-ball, as well as the rarely used basketball and football his dad bought him. He stuffed it all in a large laundry bag, and off they went.

Kim figured they'd spent a large part of the day just playing. Then she'd see how he received things; careful not to overdo it.

First to the track. "Let's walk together honey, and if you want to go faster, I'll stay with you. Ok?" Bryce started out quickly, but soon realized that wouldn't work. His pace slowed, but he was determined to continue. Kim kept a close eye on him, and marveled at his grittiness. She felt a swell in her chest, realizing that this is what he wanted. His little legs continued in a measured stride, and she wondered if he'd be able to complete a lap. Bryce said very little, other than to check on Kim. She assured him that she was fine. At the half-way mark, Bryce started to jog. Kim couldn't believe it. It wasn't much of a jog, but he was jogging nonetheless.

He looked up at her. His young round face began to fill with perspiration, and his cheeks turned a reddish hue. "You're sweating too mommy." "I am honey." Kim was thankful that he didn't notice her tears…

After a lap, they walked over to the gym bag that Kim packed, and each grabbed a water bottle. She told him over and over how proud of him she was. As they sat, she talked to him about going to school for the first time, and maybe what he could expect. Then quickly changed the subject, as she realized that once again she was being the overprotective mom. She knew that Bryce was such a sweet kid, and very likable. But kids will be kids.

"How 'bout we shoot some hoops?", Kim asked. They walked over to the basketball court where they were all alone in the morning calm – just as she had hoped. Kim showed him how to dribble the ball. They passed the ball around and had so much fun. Bryce even made a few shots into a lower basket. They laughed and played together and had so much fun. It was his best time ever, he thought. Kim was amazed at his energy. She was having as good a time as Bryce.

Following another water break, Kim took out Bryce's glove and ball and headed across the way to the baseball field. She showed him how to catch and throw, as best she could. They both agreed that he would need a lot of work; but not bad for a first day. They finished up with another lap around the track. This time, Bryce was more spirited, as he really seemed to enjoy himself. His pace was more rapid, as he made a game out of trying to pass mommy. It was all so refreshing for Kim.

They spent the rest of the morning together. Kim took Bryce grocery shopping, sure to get all the things that he would need for a healthy diet, to include the tastiest treats.

Afterwards, she noticed that Bryce was starting to wind down just a bit, and knew that it was time for lunch, followed by his nap. They'd had a great day. Bryce never complained about anything, and was grateful for the time with his mom.

I am so tired…, Bryce thought. He never dreamed his mom could be so much fun! This was his best day ever. This was what he imagined it would be like with his dad. Running, jumping and lots of laughter. Oh well. As he laid down for his nap, he dreamed of one day being as good in basketball and baseball as the older kids that play in the park. He imagined playing in a game and making lots of shots. Always the hero. Seconds later, he was fast asleep.

This routine continued over the next few weeks. Dribbling, shooting, and passing the basketball. Playing catch with his mom in the park, and jogging around the track. The results were very noticeable. Bryce was becoming very athletic and physically fit in such a short amount of time. His snacks were now completely healthy; although Kim would let him cheat from time to time. During a weekend visit, his dad couldn't get over the "new" Bryce. Kim couldn't believe her eyes as she watched his improvement each day. Bryce was able to dribble and shoot the basketball with a lot of confidence. He actually caught the baseball, fielded grounders, and threw it back to his mom with a degree of accuracy that Kim had never imagined in such a short amount of time. And he's only 6, she thought. She never had to force him to get up and go play; he enjoyed it and was having so much fun. More importantly, she learned so much about her son. Their conversations became so open and honest; they became each other's best friend.

If she lived an eternity, she told herself she would never forget one very special conversation they had. When, for whatever reason, he asked her if it mattered what people looked like. She hesitated.

"What do you mean Bryce?" she asked.

"You know. People look different.

…and I see people looking at me sometimes."

"Well… does it bother you?"

"Sometimes. They act like they've never seen a fat kid before."

Kim had no idea how to respond at that moment. So she did what came natural. She leaned over and hugged her baby as only a mother could. There were so many things going through her mind. She realized that maybe she had put so much effort into focusing on his size, that she forgot the importance of him just being himself; a very good person. In fact, he was a wonderful kid! And so smart. "Bryce". "I owe you an apology." "Honey… there are so many things I need to tell you, but the first thing is for you to know that no matter what, always be truthful. Always be honest to yourself, and those that love and care about you. And regardless of your weight, you can do anything you want to do in life. I love you so much, and I want you to be strong and healthy. And I love the time we're spending together each day. We won't be able to do this once school starts, so I'm loving these moments. And by the way, maybe people are looking at you because you are the cutest and sweetest boy ever! So when they do, just look back at them and smile. A child's smile goes a long way." Whew, she thought. Hoping it was a good response. It was the truth, so that's all she could do.

CHAPTER FOUR

Bryce was starting to feel really good about himself. He could feel his body getting stronger, and he didn't crave unhealthy snacks as he once did. He loved the time spent with his mom, and looked forward to their trips to the park. He even discovered new friends.

Bryce had noticed Brooke and Micah in the park during his past trips, but never thought to play with them. But now his confidence was growing, and he had no problem approaching them in the sand pit.

"Can I play with you guys", Bryce asked.

"Sure, what's your name", Brooke responded.

"I'm Bryce, what's yours".

"Well, I'm Brooke, and this is Micah. Is that your mom? You guys come here a lot."

The 3 of them seemed to hit it off very well from the beginning. Bryce, even though he had lost weight, was still a portly fellow; quite the opposite of Brooke and Micah, both very thin.

While the parents chatted, the three kids spent time learning about each other. They discovered that they were all the same age, and going into the first grade. Brooke and Micah were in kindergarten the previous year, while Kim kept Bryce home to teach him the basics: reading, writing, and arithmetic.

While in the park, they built sandcastles, made sand angels, and had fun doing the fun things kids do in sand. They talked about the things they liked, and the things they disliked. Bryce talked about exercising with his mom, and why he didn't eat a lot of junk food anymore. He even talked about gaining lots of weight, and not having his dad around. But that was ok, because Brooke and Micah shared as well. Brooke, like Bryce, was an only child from a single parent. Only, the parent was her dad. Her mom had passed away when she was very young. She didn't give any details, and Bryce was sure not to ask any questions about it.

Even though his mom seemed like a much better person and much more peaceful, Bryce at times wondered what it'd be like with his dad back home. Now he meets Brooke whose mom is never coming home. What must that be like? Bryce thought.

This became quite the routine, as the kids met more and more often in the park. Eventually, Brooke and Micah began to join Bryce during his workouts with his mom. They made a fun time of it, but Kim made sure Bryce was working hard. School would start soon, and she wanted to make sure she took advantage of every moment she had with him. They played basketball; tossed the baseball; and threw the football around. Laughing all the while. At times, Bryce would stop to watch the older kids play; still amazed at their skills. He found himself trying to do some of the things they did with the basketball, which was all so very difficult… except for dribbling.

He seemed to have a knack for it. Bryce dribbled daily; either at the park or at home. Kim noticed that he constantly had a ball in his hands, and was becoming quite good.

He also developed pretty good skills at throwing and catching the football. Even more important, she thought, he was having fun with it. She could never have imagined he'd be at this point when they started this workout plan. He was having so much fun with Brooke and Micah. They were having fun as well. During their conversations at night, Kim noticed that Bryce had a new confidence about himself. He seemed surer of himself, which is all she ever wanted.

CHAPTER FIVE

During one of their park visits, Bryce noticed a sign:

TACKLE FOOTBALL TRYOUTS

WOODBRIDGE YOUTH SPORTS

AGES 5-13; SIGN UP TODAY!!

Bryce knew very little about the rules of football, or about any requirements. His dad never really talked to him about it, and showed no interest in watching games on television. What little he knew, he picked up from watching the older kids play in the park. Now he sees where there are tryouts. Tryouts? Not exactly sure what that all means, he decides to ask his mom. "What does that mean mom?" he asks. "What is tackle football?" At that point, Kim does her best to explain the basic rule of football; of which, she knows very little. "Well, one team has the ball and tries to score touchdowns, while the other team tries to stop them. The way to stop them is to tackle them and slam them to the ground… or something like that. Just like they play in the park honey." Then she went on to explain to him that there were teams for kids in different age groups, and that the kids wear uniforms, and pads, and have coaches, and blah, blah, blah…

Bryce was intrigued. Football may be just the thing to show off his new found confidence. Just hearing his mom describe it was exciting. Now Kim's thinking that maybe this isn't the best idea. She knows very little about football, and Bryce knows even less. Nevertheless, she gives in to her only child, and finds out more about this tryout.

Of course she mentions it to Brooke and Micah's parents at their parent park rendezvous. She finds out that Micah's dad has already signed him up for football, and Brooke is registered as a cheerleader. She also finds out about the Woodbridge Youth Sports Center (WYSC), and how to register for sports.

That afternoon, after their park visit, Kim and Bryce headed for the WYSC to get more information, and to maybe register Bryce for football. Once there, they got all the information they needed. Kim registered Bryce for the ankle biter 6-7 year old league, and was informed that practice would begin the following week. She was also told that the coach of the team, Coach Bonkers, would be calling with details.

Kim and Bryce continued their park visits over the next few days. Bryce was especially motivated knowing that he was trying out for football with his friend Micah. Like Bryce, Micah had never played tackle football before, but was very good at throwing and catching. He was also very fast. Throwing the football in the park meant so much more now, Bryce thought. Even pal Brooke joined in during their park "drills".

Kim remembered watching football games in high school and college, but never *really* learned all the rules. She knew he'd learn from the coaches, but to be on the safe side, she researched "this thing called tackle football", so she'd know what to expect.

Finally, the call came. Coach Bonkers called to notify Kim that practice would start on Monday, and to be there early to get his equipment. She asked what he needed to bring, and wear. "Shorts, T-shirt, and a good attitude", he stated; "and cleats if he has them." Kim spoke with the coach a little more regarding Bryce, letting him know that Bryce was new at this sports thing, and that her biggest fear was that he'd somehow get hurt. The coach assured her that most of the kids in this age group are new to tackle football. And that they'd all learn the game together. He also assured her that his intent was to make sure all the kids had fun. That put Kim's mind at ease.

The coach also told Kim that there'd be a lot of running involved during practices. He needed to get the kids in shape, so they could be at their best during games. She told him about Bryce's weight, and the workouts they'd done. She didn't think the running would be a problem at all.

So… football practice starts next week, school for Bryce starts the following week, and Kim's new job would begin the week after that. What started out as a rough time for the family following Kim and Bill's divorce, has now blossomed into the best time ever. Kim was so happy just thinking about what had transpired with Bryce in just over a month's time. Her baby was growing up; she could see it in everything he did. He spent less time in his room, and more time conversing with his mom, and watching the occasional television program in the living room. He seemed to be less of a loner, and more of a people person. Kim watched his interactions with Brooke and Micah, and Bryce always seemed to be in charge of their little group.

Making decisions about what they'd do, and how the games were played. Even though she'd spend time talking to other parents in the park, Kim was sure to keep a sharp ear and a watchful eye on Bryce. This was all new to her as well. She didn't know what to expect from him once he started interacting. Needless to say, she was very proud of Bryce, and wondered why she hadn't seen these qualities in him before. Everything he's doing at this point is so natural and effortless. Certainly not a shy boy, and very confident. Kim hoped this would define his personality as he grew older. She liked what she saw…

CHAPTER SIX

Kim and Bryce had gone to the mall together in the past, but this was a very special weekend visit. Bryce needed school clothes for the very first time, and Kim thought that maybe it was time for an upgrade from toddler outfits. Going to school as a first grader, he needed to be impressive, Kim thought. Needless to say, this was all new to her. They went to several outlets. Some notable, and some not so much. They bought jackets, shirts, short pants, regular pants, sweatshirts, and different kinds of shoes – dress and sneakers. Kim received Bryce's supply list from school, so they had to purchase lots of school items as well. Kim never imagined how much fun it would be. She and Bryce had become such great friends, and this trip made that clear. They shopped and shared a meal at the food court. Bryce played with other kids in the Kiddy Area, and they even found time for video games at Video-Rama. Bryce was thinking it was "another" best day ever. It was a very long day, only complete once Kim and Bryce took a trip to the Sporting Goods store.

Kim told the clerk that Bryce was playing football for the first time, and before she knew it, he was offering suggestions on equipment. "So… you're a football player, huh?", asked the sales clerk, rather loudly. "Well…" Bryce tried to respond, but was quickly cut off by the clerk. "We're gonna have to get you into the best stuff in the house." The clerk was a fast talker, and begin to offer up item after item. Football cleats, pants, jersey, elbow pads, knee pads, gloves, hand warmers, and all the things a new player needs to be safe and successful on the field. The sales clerk seemed excited about the possibility of a big sell. Luckily, Kim had already talked to the coach, and knew exactly what Bryce would need. "That's all so nice, but we'll just go with cleats today", she said. "Maybe shorts and t-shirts too". Bryce was so excited trying on the football cleats. He noticed other kids about his age getting cleats as well. Kim was doubly excited just watching her son. What a wonderful experience! She also had to think about how Bill was missing out… oh well.

On Sunday morning, the day after the mall visit, Bryce wanted to wear his new cleats outside. Kim thought it'd be ok after church. She called Micah's mom to see if maybe they could join them in the park. She thought it was a great idea. Just to be on the safe side, Kim called Brooke's dad to let him know their plans as well. He didn't think they'd make it, but hoped they'd have fun.

Kim finally told Bryce that yes, he could wear his new cleats to the park to get used to them, but he absolutely had to behave in church that morning. Not that he ever really misbehaved, but Kim just liked knowing she had leverage.

Bryce was sure to have one of his healthy snacks for breakfast. He never complained about his meals, and knew all too well that everything he was doing was for the best. Kim was sure to weigh him and measure his height once a week – always on Sunday. It became such a big deal to them. Having to wait and see if there's any change, and if so, how much? Is all this exercise paying off? Is she doing right by his diet? Kim had so many questions, but felt in her heart she was doing the right thing by her son. Feeling it was one thing; seeing it on the scales was another. The weekly anticipation to see if he'd lost weight was terrible, she thought. But always fun afterwards. Especially if the loss was significant. Which it had been in recent weeks. This week was no different. Bryce had lost a considerable amount of weight in the short time since they started this process. Kim was sure to explain to him that she imagined he would be happier and healthier if he was to lose some the weight he was carrying around, but that people can be just as happy with the weight. She also explained to him that what's important is how you feel about yourself, and not what others think about you. There were so many life lessons there, and Kim didn't wanna confuse Bryce at such a young age. She hoped the total change in his behavior and attitude were good signs…

Church was great! Everyone talked about the changes in Bryce. Especially how he decided against the unhealthy snacks that were in the common area. Chocolates; cupcakes; crackers; cookies; and an assortment of candies were all about. Sooooo very tempting, thought Bryce. Oddly enough, it seemed that the less junk food he ate, the less he wanted.

Bryce could hardly wait to get home and get his cleats for the park. He was so excited. True to her word, Kim was eager to get him there. But first, they'd have to circle the track as part of their workout routine. So Bryce put his cleats in the gym bag with all the other items, and off they went. Along the way, they had the usual conversations about school, his dad, football, and whatever else came up. Football practice would start the next day. "Are you ready"? Kim asked. "I guess. Is dad gonna be there?" "I honestly don't know honey. Coach Bonkers said you'd run a lot…"

As they got closer to the park, Bryce could see all the people out doing different things. He noticed a lady he'd seen often walking her Labrador retriever. "Mom, when can I get a dog?" "When you're older. We've already talked about that." "What about a bicycle? Micah's getting one for his birthday." "Hmmm… we'll see about that." Not a bad idea, thought Kim.

Once at the track, they began their routine. Kim started with a slow trot, and Bryce would run with her. At some point, she picks up her pace, and Bryce continues on his own. When he can no longer run, he picks up a fast walk. Sure to keep moving. Just as they were finishing up, Bryce could see Micah's mom pulling into the parking lot. He was tired, but really happy to see his buddy. Micah and Brooke were his first real friends… ONLY friends. "Mom. They're here!" "I see them", Kim responded.

For the next few hours, the ladies talked about so many things, including football, school, and the kids. They were becoming very good friends. Bryce and Micah were having the time of their lives. They started out throwing the football around. They were both getting really good at catching and throwing. After a while, they took out the basketball and dribbled around the court. The mom's helped with a little 2 on 2. They finished up by playing catch with the baseball, and practicing hitting using the plastic bat and ball set Micah's mom brought to the park. Again, the mom's joined in. What fun!

After a while, it was time to call it a day. The ladies talked about seeing each other the next day at football practice, and what to bring to ward off pesky insects and too much sun.

At home, Kim prepared a healthy meal for the two of them, and later settled down to watch one of Bryce's favorite television shows. Kim was sure to text Bill about Bryce's practice. Bill was genuinely excited, but didn't know if he could make it on Monday. Bryce was a little disappointed when Kim told him, but he understood.

That night, while lying in bed, Bryce was filled with excitement and anticipation of what the next day would bring. He didn't know what to expect, and he didn't care. He just knew that he would get the chance to play football on a team. Having Micah there made it even more special, he thought. Eventually, his excitement became exhaustion, and Bryce was asleep before he knew it…

CHAPTER SEVEN

The day started uneventful, as Bryce got up and enjoyed himself a nourishing breakfast. Kim had errands to run so she got him dressed, and off they went. No fun at the park today because Kim knew Bryce would need to conserve his energy for practice later in the day. At least according to the coach. Once they returned home from her errands, both Bryce and Kim just lounged around waiting until it was time to leave. It was gonna be a hot day, so Bryce put on his new shorts and a tee-shirt. Kim was sure to bring plenty of water, a towel, and a change of clothes, just in case. Bryce tends to sweat a lot.

Once they arrived at the field, there was a lot of confusion, with so many kids running around, and so many parents trying to figure out where they were supposed to go. Luckily, Coach Bonkers had explained to all the parents of his team that at least 5 different teams were meeting there for the first time and this was to be expected. He also told them that he would wear a red cap and a matching tee-shirt; that would certainly help to locate him.

Bryce spotted Coach Bonkers before Kim did. They walked over and stood amongst the throng of kids and parents surrounding the coach. Micah and his mom eventually worked their way through the crowd, and met up with Kim and Bryce. Bryce and Micah didn't say too much, but were busy watching the other kids, assuming they'd all be teammates. Coach Bonkers started off by introducing himself and two assistant coaches. "Hey everyone.

I'm Coach Bonkers, and this is Coach Banner", pointing to a somewhat hefty fellow; "and Coach Blame", a younger smaller version of Coach Banner. "I want all the ankle-biter Eagles to go with Coach Banner. He's gonna work you through some exercises to get you all going. Parents, if you could just stay here for our first meeting, that'd be great." "LET'S GO EAGLES!!" screamed Coach Banner, as he ran to a different part of the field, about 20 kids in tow. Bryce and Micah ran behind Coach Banner, and were able to stay with him, unlike a lot of the other kids. Coach Banner gave the kids a rah-rah pep talk, had them run around the field, do push-ups, and run through a number of football drills. After about 15 minutes or so, once he was done with the parents, Coach Bonkers joined them and gave them his own pep talk. Then they ran some more. Bryce was tired, but not nearly as tired as some of the other kids. Even though he was still a bit heavy, he was in very good physical shape. All the work he and Kim put in during the previous 6 weeks was paying off. He knew it. Bryce was so proud of himself, as he ran through all the drills. Coach Bonkers and Coach Banner continued to call out his name, and tell him he was doing a great job. "Way to go Bryce! Great job!" When the team took laps around the field, Bryce and Micah were always near the front. It was only the first day, but the two of them stood out from the other kids. Bryce was sure to locate Kim and give her a look whenever he could. He was so happy, she thought.

There was a moment, however, when Bryce looked over and didn't see his mom. He wasn't worried. He knew she was there.

What he didn't know, was that Kim had excused herself from Micah's mom, and gone briefly back to her car. Watching her son this day, and seeing what he'd become in just a few months, unleashed emotions that she couldn't contain. She started weeping while watching him, and ran to her car to cry some more. She thought about how proud she was of him. Beyond proud! She wished she could share that moment with Bill, but realized that it didn't matter. This was about Bryce, and how he decided he wanted to make a change.

Wow! Kim thought. All this after a half day of football practice. What's gonna happen when school starts next week? Or if he plays basketball and baseball? I guess I'll just have to wait and see. Stay tuned...

TO BE CONTINUED...

Look for "Life With Bryce 2: The Season Begins"

LIFE WITH BRYCE: A MOTHER'S LOVE

BOOK DESCRIPTION

Young Bryce Johnson had no friends, and no real desires, other than hanging out in his room, watching television, playing with his toys, and eating lots of snacks. To make matters worse, Bryce was the only child of divorced parents who were too consumed with their own concerns, and not much thought towards nurturing and encouragement for Bryce. In the meantime, Bryce gained weight at an alarming rate, seemingly unnoticed by his parents. Once the dust settled, Bryce's mom knew it was up to her to refocus her attention on her son, and rebuild his self- confidence. Will Bryce be up to the task?

LIFE WITH BRYCE: A MOTHER'S LOVE

AUTHOR DESCRIPTION

As a father, coach, and educator, the author has lived or been a part of the lives of the characters of which he writes. He has seen first-hand the problems young kids encounter and how they respond, particularly without adult intervention. The author pens stories about such encounters, and hopes that the reader becomes educated on the hopes, dreams, and realities of someone so young. The children are our future and should not be ignored.

Printed in the United States
By Bookmasters